D0603945

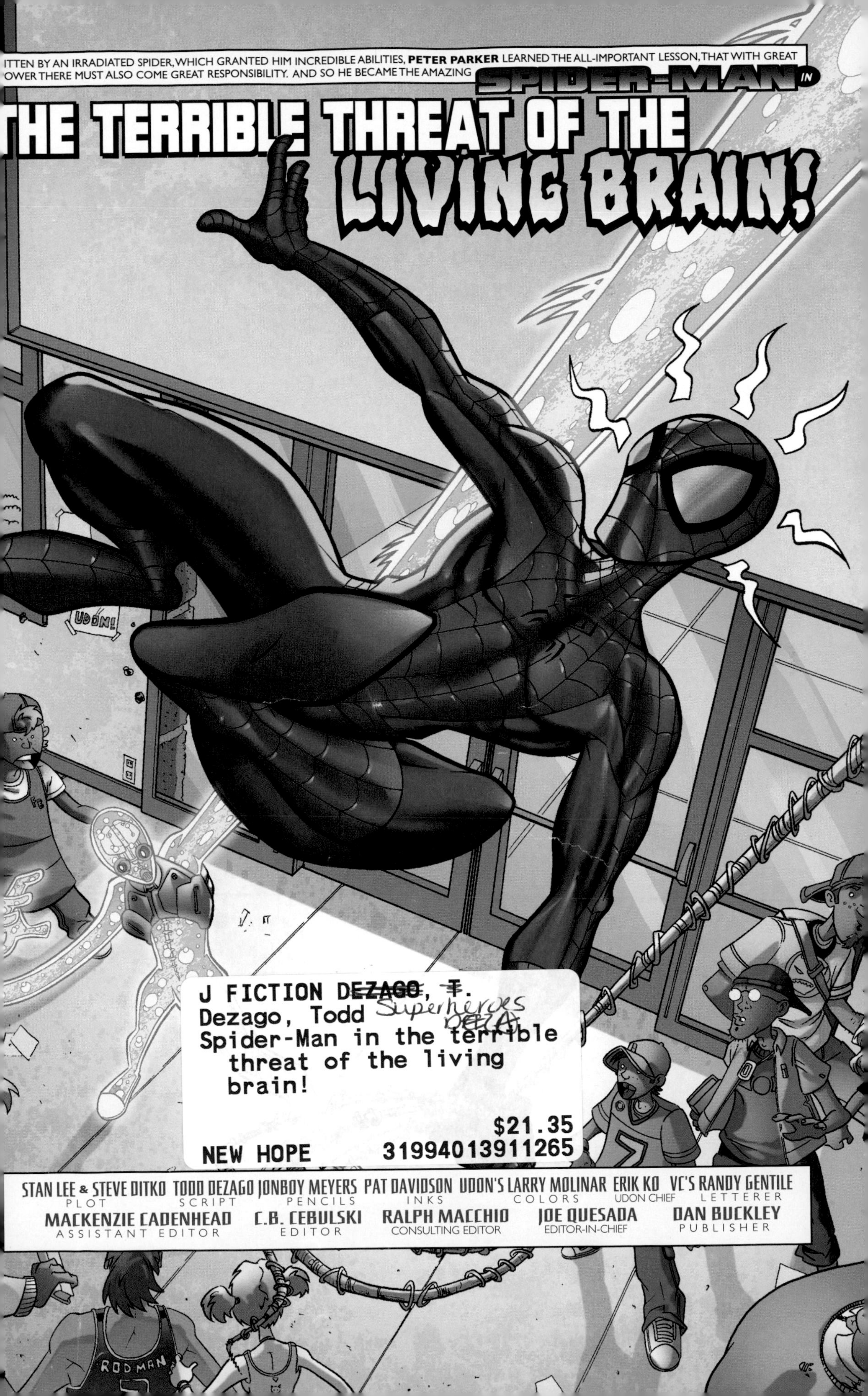
ITTEN BY AN IRRADIATED SPIDER, WHICH GRANTED HIM INCREDIBLE ABILITIES, PETER PARKER LEARNED THE ALL-IMPORTANT LESSON, THAT WITH GREAT OWER THERE MUST ALSO COME GREAT RESPONSIBILITY. AND SO HE BECAME THE AMAZING SPIDER-MAN IN
THE TERRIBLE THREAT OF THE LIVING BRAIN!
UDÖN!
STAN LEE & STEVE DITKO PLOT
TODD DEZAGO SCRIPT
JONBOY MEYERS PENCILS
PAT DAVIDSON INKS
UDON'S LARRY MOLINAR COLORS
ERIK KO UDON CHIEF
VC'S RANDY GENTILE LETTERER
MACKENZIE CADENHEAD ASSISTANT EDITOR
C.B. CEBULSKI EDITOR
RALPH MACCHIO CONSULTING EDITOR
JOE QUESADA EDITOR-IN-CHIEF
DAN BUCKLEY PUBLISHER
RODMAN

VISIT US AT
www.abdopublishing.com

Spotlight, a division of ABDO Publishing Company Inc., is the school and library distributor of the Marvel Entertainment books.

Library of Congress Cataloging-in-Publication Data

Dezago, Todd.
   The terrible threat of the living brain! / Stan Lee & Steve Ditko, plot ; Todd Dezago, script ; Jonboy Meyers, pencils ; Pat Davidson, inks ; Larry Molinar, colors ; Erik Ko, Udon chief ; Randy Gentile, letterer. -- Library bound ed.
     p. cm. -- (Spider-Man)
   "Marvel age"--Cover.
   Revision of the July 2004 issue of Marvel age Spider-Man.
   ISBN-13: 978-1-59961-008-5
   ISBN-10: 1-59961-008-6
   1. Graphic novels. I. Lee, Stan. II. Ditko, Steve. III. Meyers, Jonboy. IV. Marvel age Spider-Man. V. Title. VI. Title: Terrible threat of the living brain! VII. Series: Spider-Man (Series)

PN6728.S6D535 2006
741.5'973--dc22

                                                    2006043463

All Spotlight books are reinforced library binding and manufactured in the United States of America.

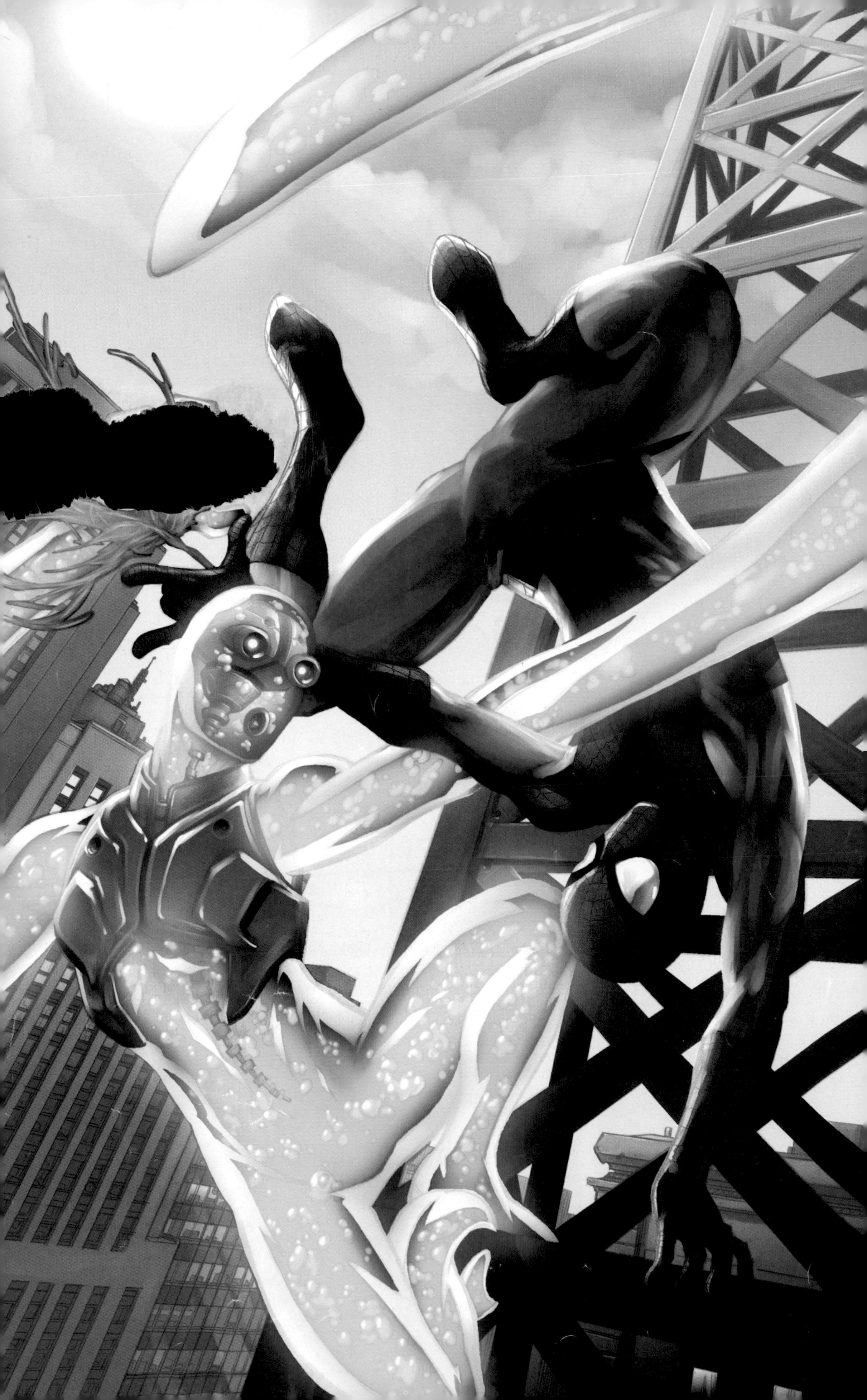

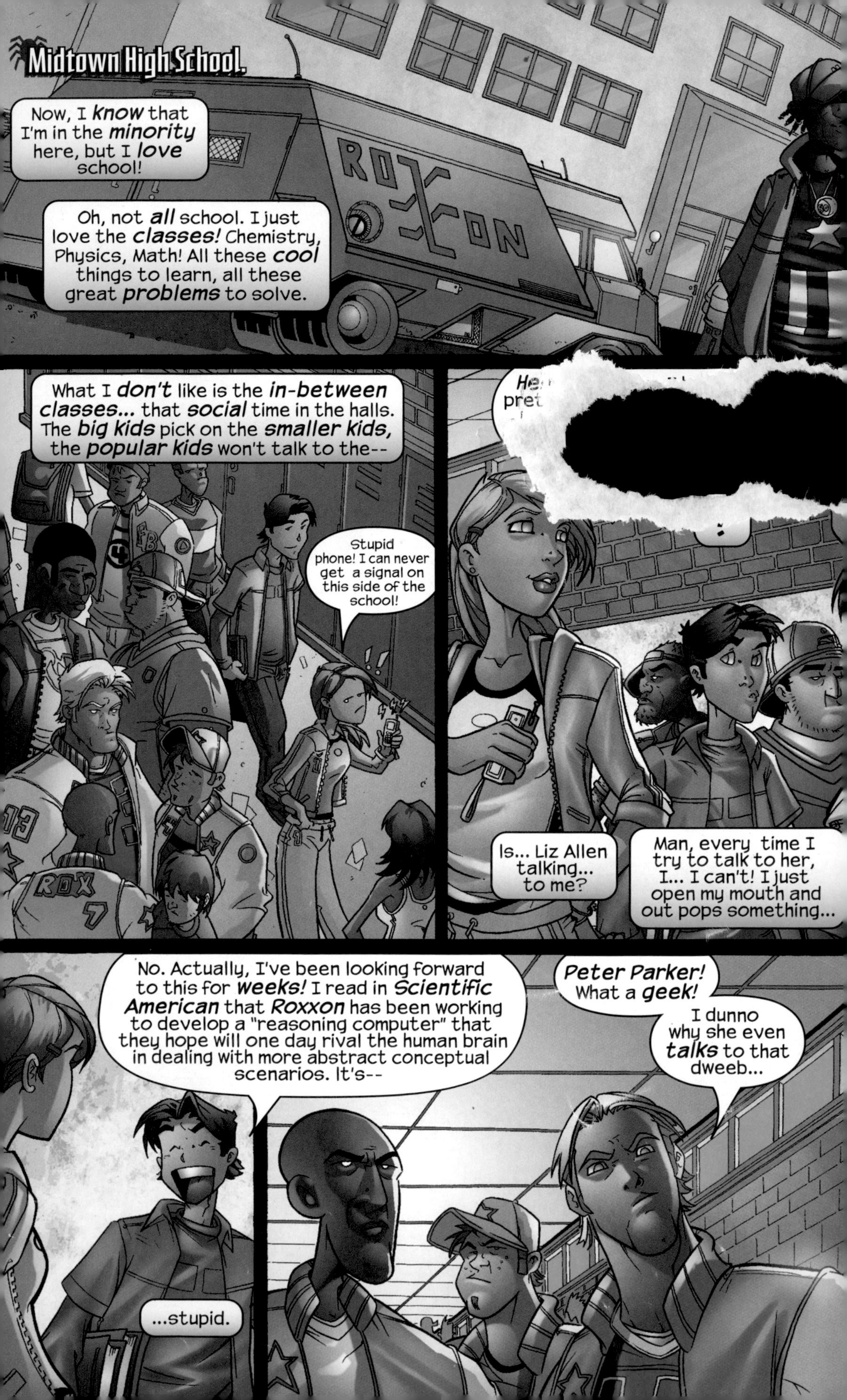
Midtown High School.
Now, I know that I'm in the minority here, but I love school!
Oh, not all school. I just love the classes! Chemistry, Physics, Math! All these cool things to learn, all these great problems to solve.
ROXXON
What I don't like is the in-between classes... that social time in the halls. The big kids pick on the smaller kids, the popular kids won't talk to the--
Stupid phone! I can never get a signal on this side of the school!
[redacted]
Is... Liz Allen talking... to me?
Man, every time I try to talk to her, I... I can't! I just open my mouth and out pops something...
No. Actually, I've been looking forward to this for weeks! I read in Scientific American that Roxxon has been working to develop a "reasoning computer" that they hope will one day rival the human brain in dealing with more abstract conceptual scenarios. It's--
...stupid.
Peter Parker! What a geek!
I dunno why she even talks to that dweeb...

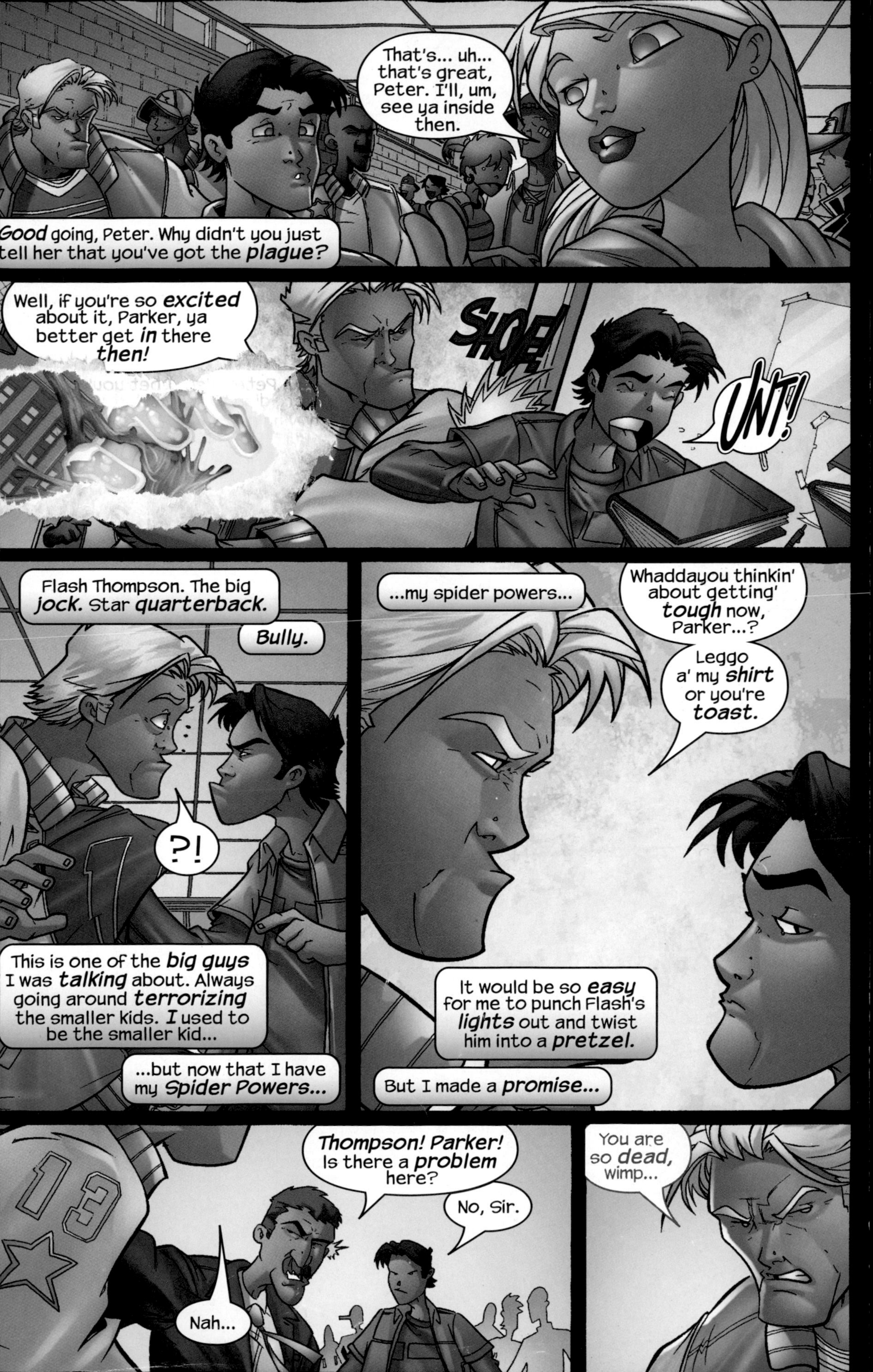

That's... uh... that's great, Peter. I'll, um, see ya inside then.
Good going, Peter. Why didn't you just tell her that you've got the plague?
Well, if you're so excited about it, Parker, ya better get in there then!
SHOVE!
UNT!
Flash Thompson. The big jock. Star quarterback.
Bully.
?!
This is one of the big guys I was talking about. Always going around terrorizing the smaller kids. I used to be the smaller kid...
...but now that I have my Spider Powers...
...my spider powers...
Whaddayou thinkin' about getting' tough now, Parker...?
Leggo a' my shirt or you're toast.
It would be so easy for me to punch Flash's lights out and twist him into a pretzel.
But I made a promise...
Thompson! Parker! Is there a problem here?
No, Sir.
Nah...
You are so dead, wimp...

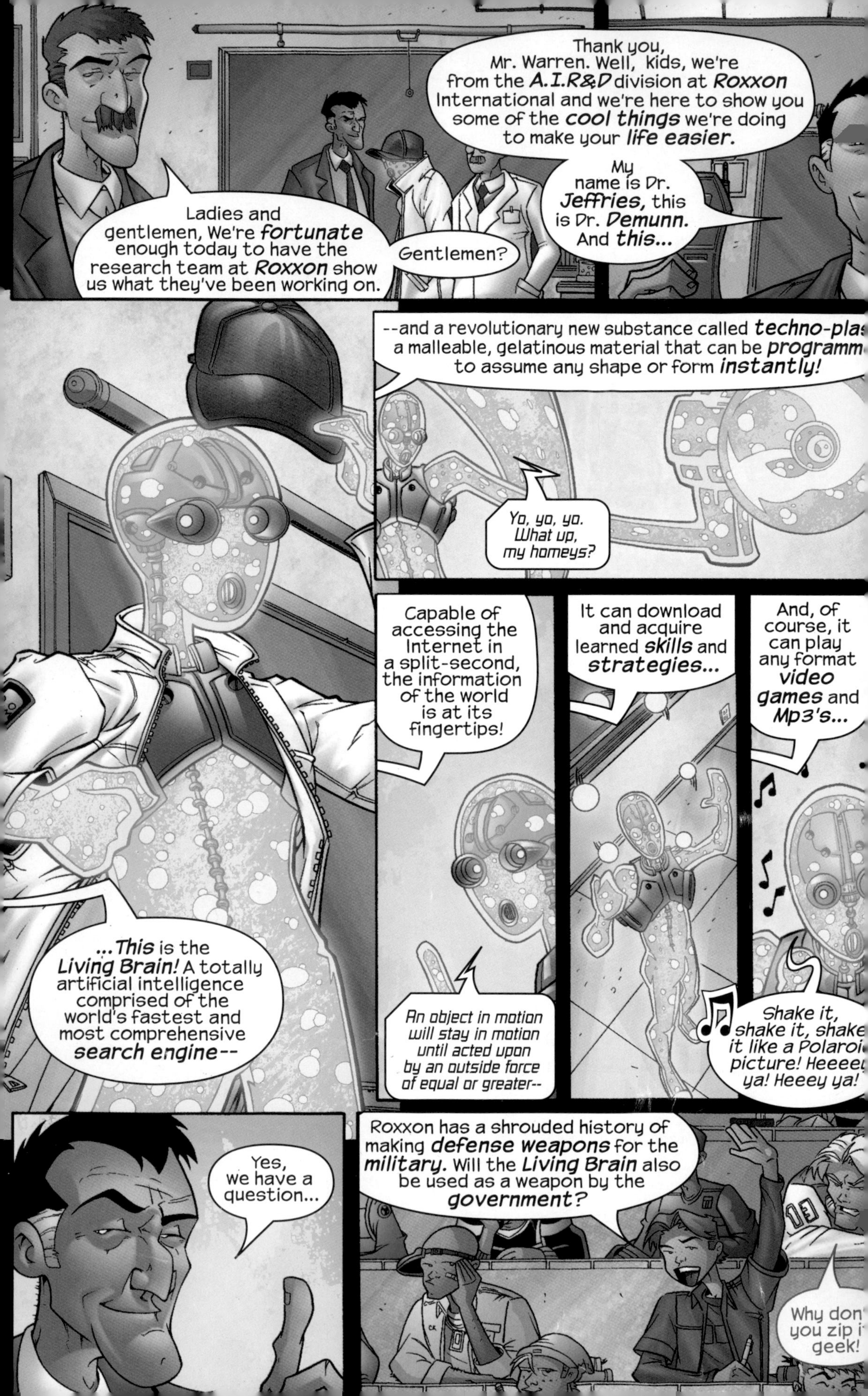

Thank you, Mr. Warren. Well, kids, we're from the A.I.R&D division at Roxxon International and we're here to show you some of the cool things we're doing to make your life easier.
Ladies and gentlemen, We're fortunate enough today to have the research team at Roxxon show us what they've been working on.
Gentlemen?
My name is Dr. Jeffries, this is Dr. Demunn. And this...
...This is the Living Brain! A totally artificial intelligence comprised of the world's fastest and most comprehensive search engine--
--and a revolutionary new substance called techno-plas
a malleable, gelatinous material that can be programm
to assume any shape or form instantly!
Yo, yo, yo. What up, my homeys?
Capable of accessing the Internet in a split-second, the information of the world is at its fingertips!
An object in motion will stay in motion until acted upon by an outside force of equal or greater--
It can download and acquire learned skills and strategies...
And, of course, it can play any format video games and Mp3's...
Shake it, shake it, shake it like a Polaroi picture! Heeeei ya! Heeey ya!
Yes, we have a question...
Roxxon has a shrouded history of making defense weapons for the military. Will the Living Brain also be used as a weapon by the government?
Why don you zip i geek!

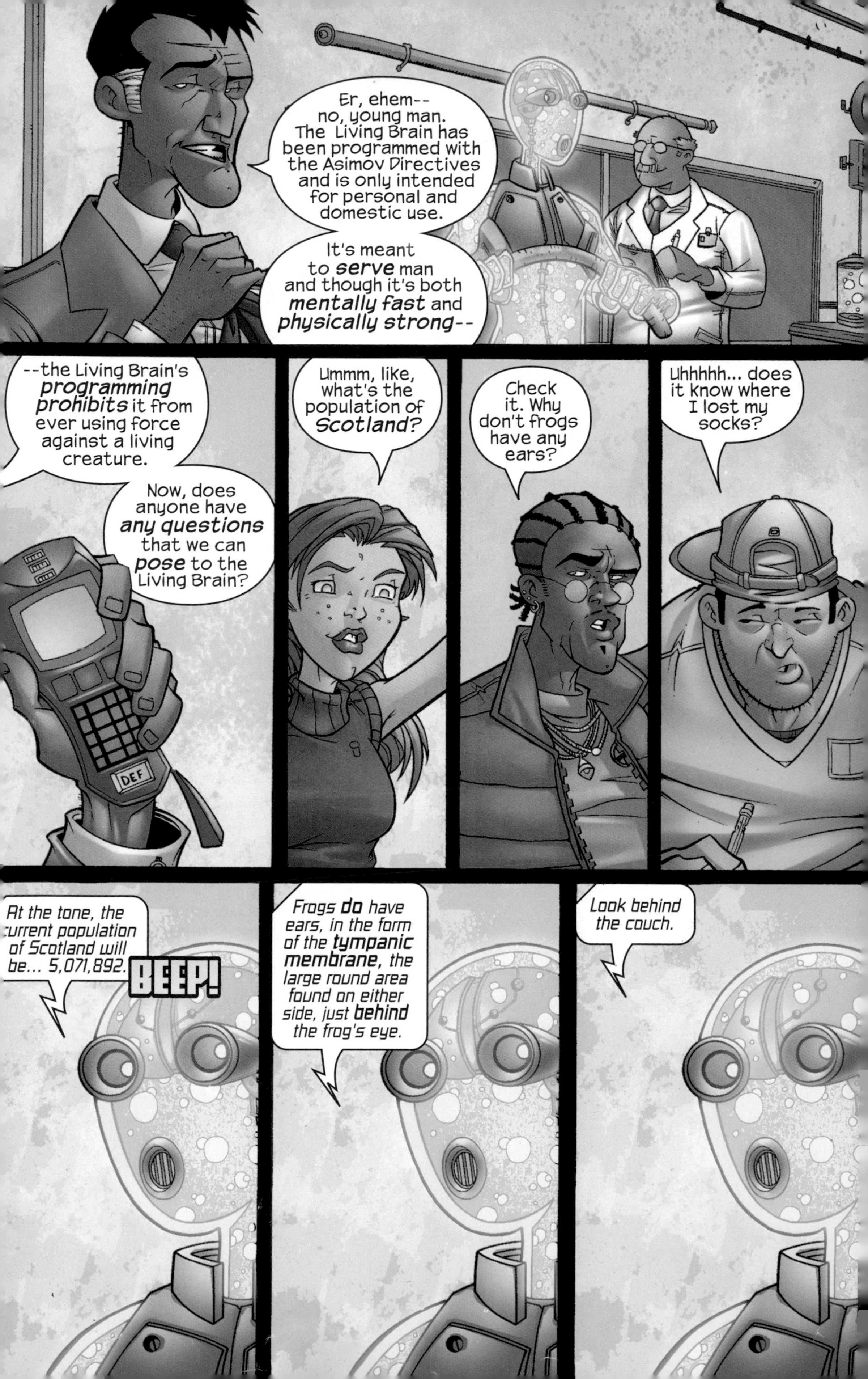
Er, ehem-- no, young man. The Living Brain has been programmed with the Asimov Directives and is only intended for personal and domestic use.
It's meant to **serve** man and though it's both **mentally fast** and **physically strong**--
--the Living Brain's **programming prohibits** it from ever using force against a living creature.
Now, does anyone have **any questions** that we can **pose** to the Living Brain?
DEF
Ummm, like, what's the population of **Scotland?**
Check it. Why don't frogs have any ears?
Uhhhhh... does it know where I lost my socks?
At the tone, the current population of Scotland will be... 5,071,892.
BEEP!
Frogs **do** have ears, in the form of the **tympanic membrane**, the large round area found on either side, just **behind** the frog's eye.
Look behind the couch.

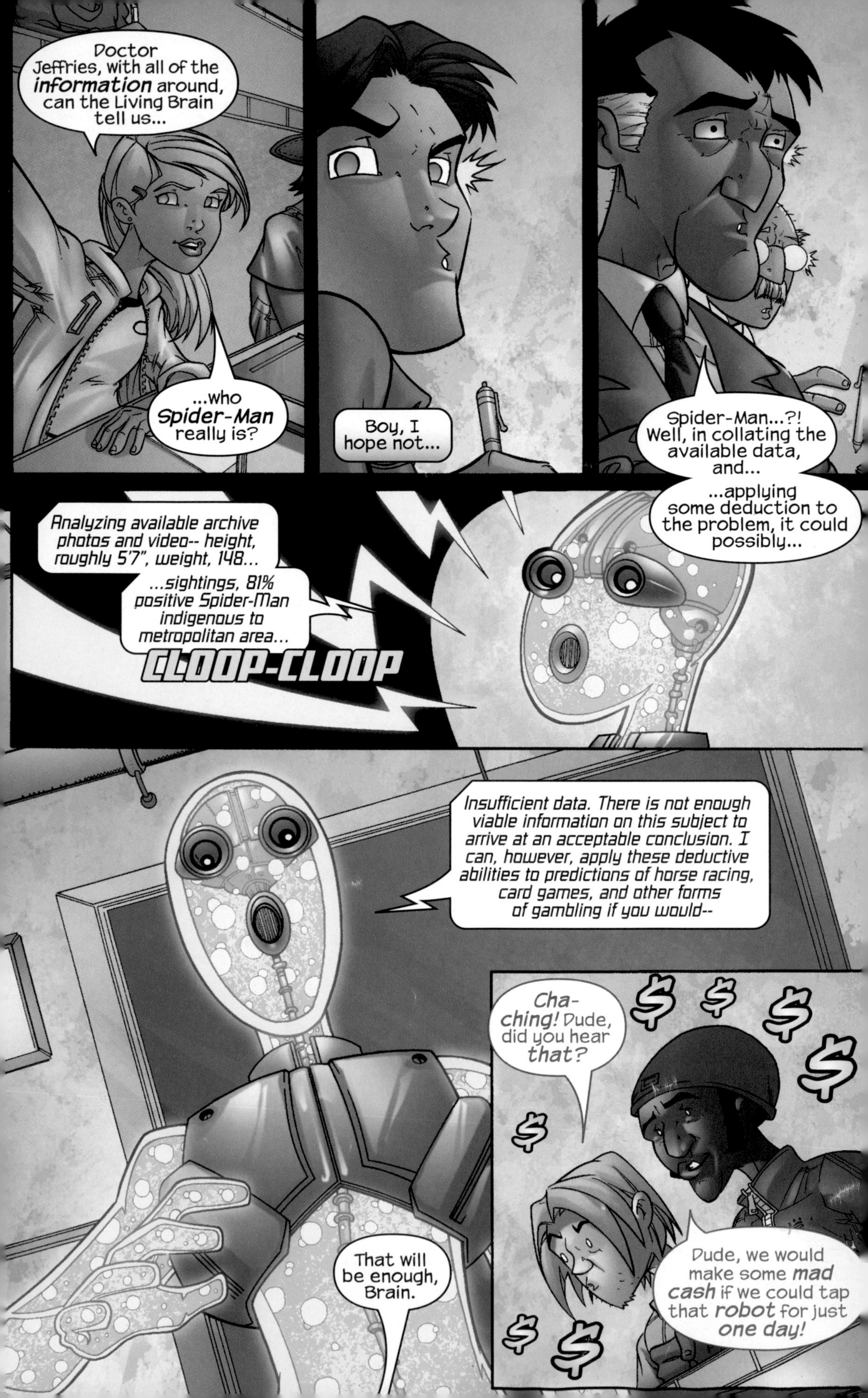

Doctor Jeffries, with all of the information around, can the Living Brain tell us...
...who Spider-Man really is?
Boy, I hope not...
Spider-Man...?! Well, in collating the available data, and...
...applying some deduction to the problem, it could possibly...
Analyzing available archive photos and video-- height, roughly 5'7", weight, 148...
...sightings, 81% positive Spider-Man indigenous to metropolitan area...
CLOOP-CLOOP
Insufficient data. There is not enough viable information on this subject to arrive at an acceptable conclusion. I can, however, apply these deductive abilities to predictions of horse racing, card games, and other forms of gambling if you would--
That will be enough, Brain.
Cha-ching! Dude, did you hear that?
Dude, we would make some mad cash if we could tap that robot for just one day!

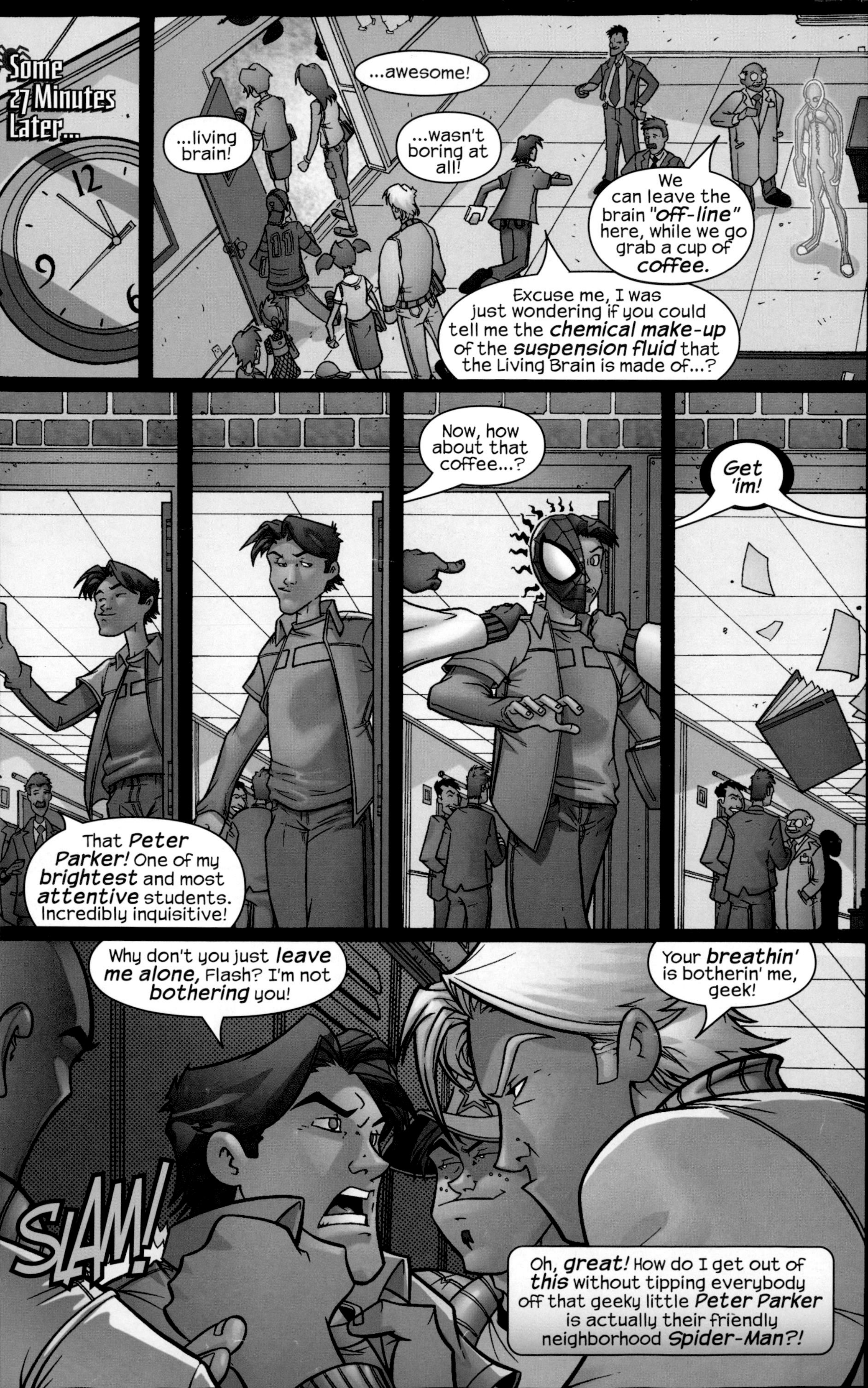
Some 27 Minutes Later...
...living brain!
...awesome!
...wasn't boring at all!
We can leave the brain "off-line" here, while we go grab a cup of coffee.
Excuse me, I was just wondering if you could tell me the chemical make-up of the suspension fluid that the Living Brain is made of...?
That Peter Parker! One of my brightest and most attentive students. Incredibly inquisitive!
Now, how about that coffee...?
Get 'im!
Why don't you just leave me alone, Flash? I'm not bothering you!
Your breathin' is botherin' me, geek!
SLAM!
Oh, great! How do I get out of this without tipping everybody off that geeky little Peter Parker is actually their friendly neighborhood Spider-Man?!

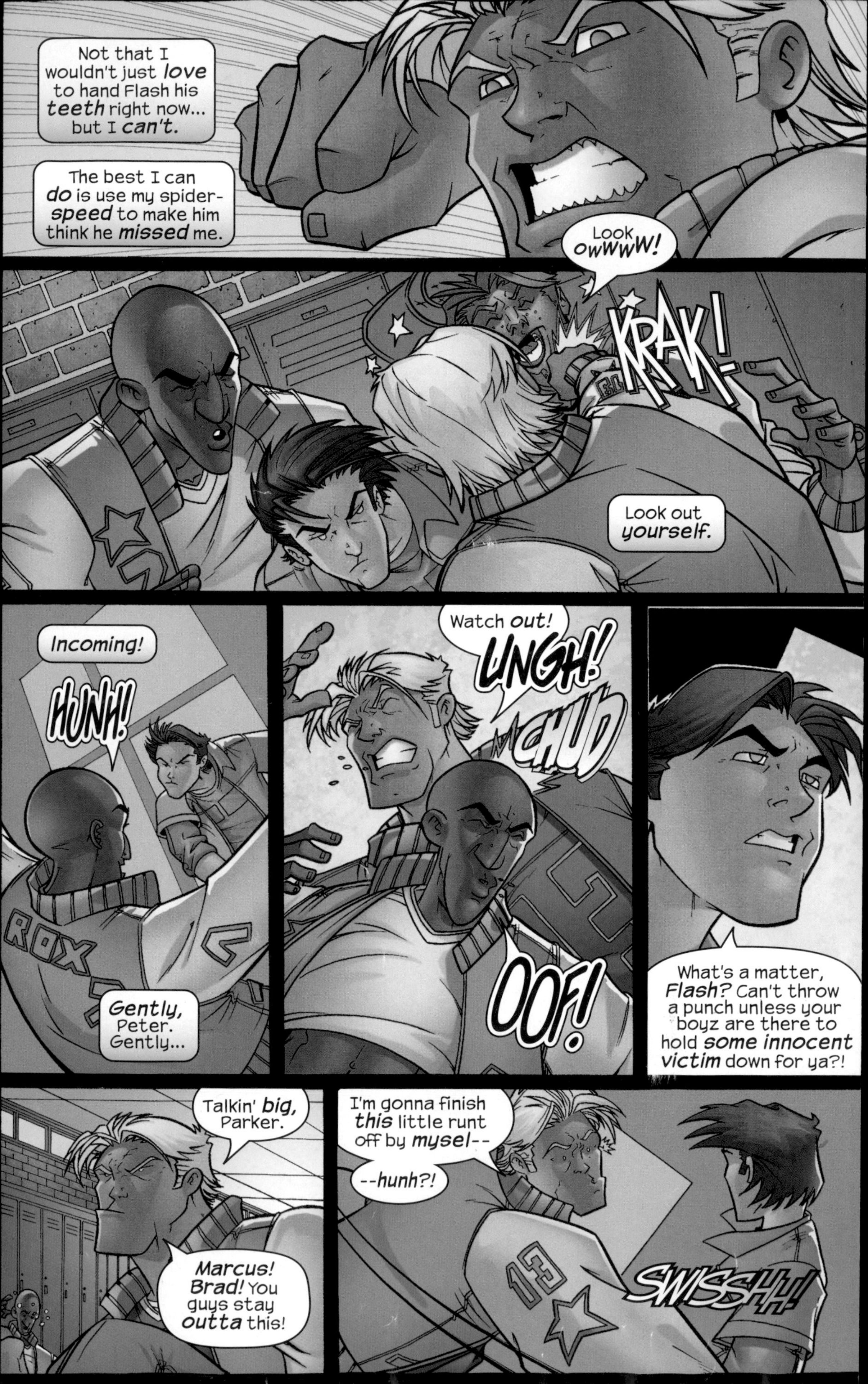
Not that I wouldn't just love to hand Flash his teeth right now... but I can't.
The best I can do is use my spider-speed to make him think he missed me.
Look owwwW!
KRAK!
Look out yourself.
Incoming!
HUNH!
Gently, Peter. Gently...
Watch out!
UNGH!
CHUD
OOF!
What's a matter, Flash? Can't throw a punch unless your boyz are there to hold some innocent victim down for ya?!
Talkin' big, Parker.
Marcus! Brad! You guys stay outta this!
I'm gonna finish this little runt off by mysel--
--hunh?!
SWISSH!

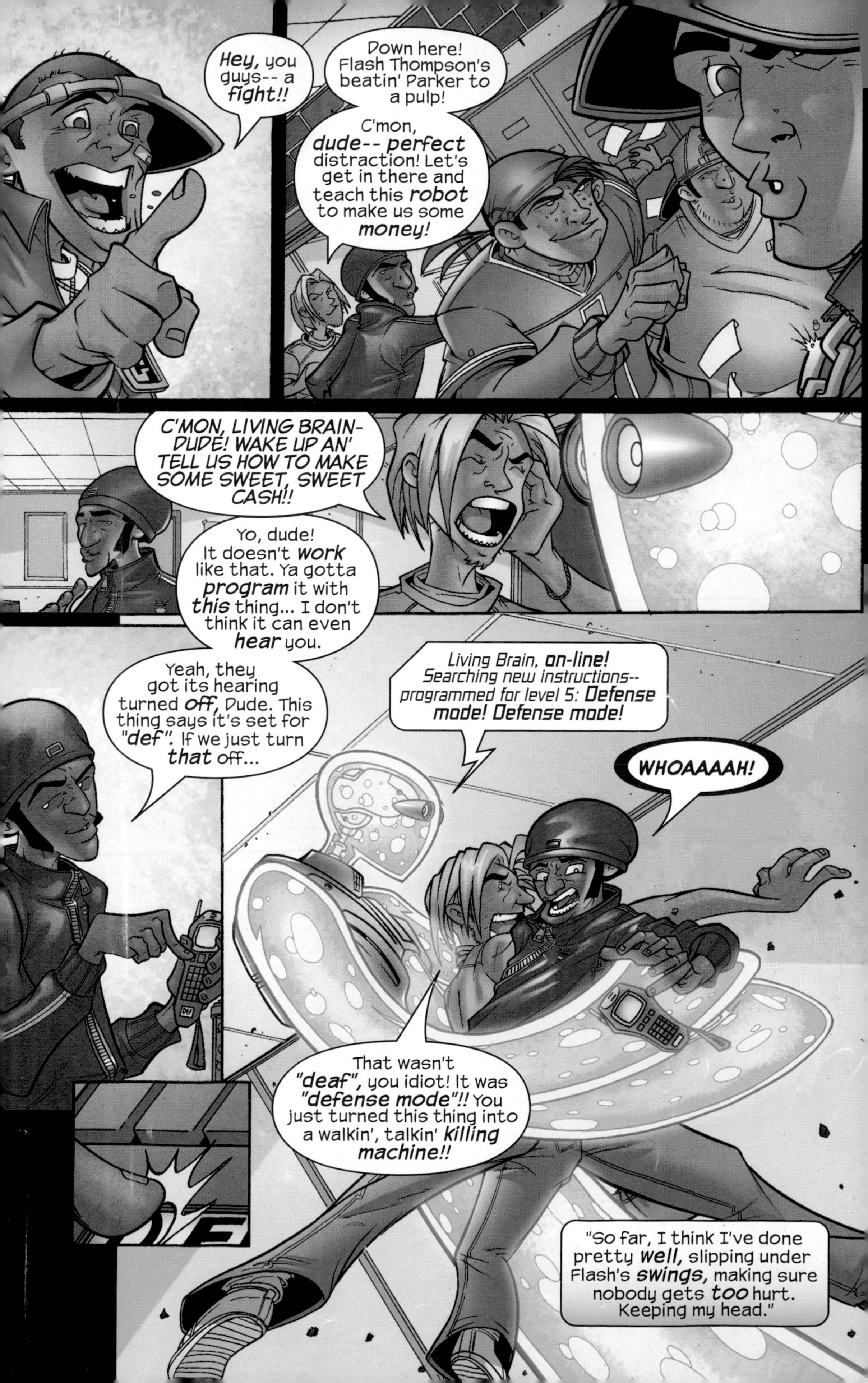
Hey, you guys-- a fight!!
Down here! Flash Thompson's beatin' Parker to a pulp!
C'mon, dude-- perfect distraction! Let's get in there and teach this robot to make us some money!
C'MON, LIVING BRAIN-DUDE! WAKE UP AN' TELL US HOW TO MAKE SOME SWEET, SWEET CASH!!
Yo, dude! It doesn't work like that. Ya gotta program it with this thing... I don't think it can even hear you.
Yeah, they got its hearing turned off, Dude. This thing says it's set for "def". If we just turn that off...
Living Brain, on-line! Searching new instructions-- programmed for level 5: Defense mode! Defense mode!
WHOAAAAH!
That wasn't "deaf", you idiot! It was "defense mode"!! You just turned this thing into a walkin', talkin' killing machine!!
"So far, I think I've done pretty well, slipping under Flash's swings, making sure nobody gets too hurt. Keeping my head."

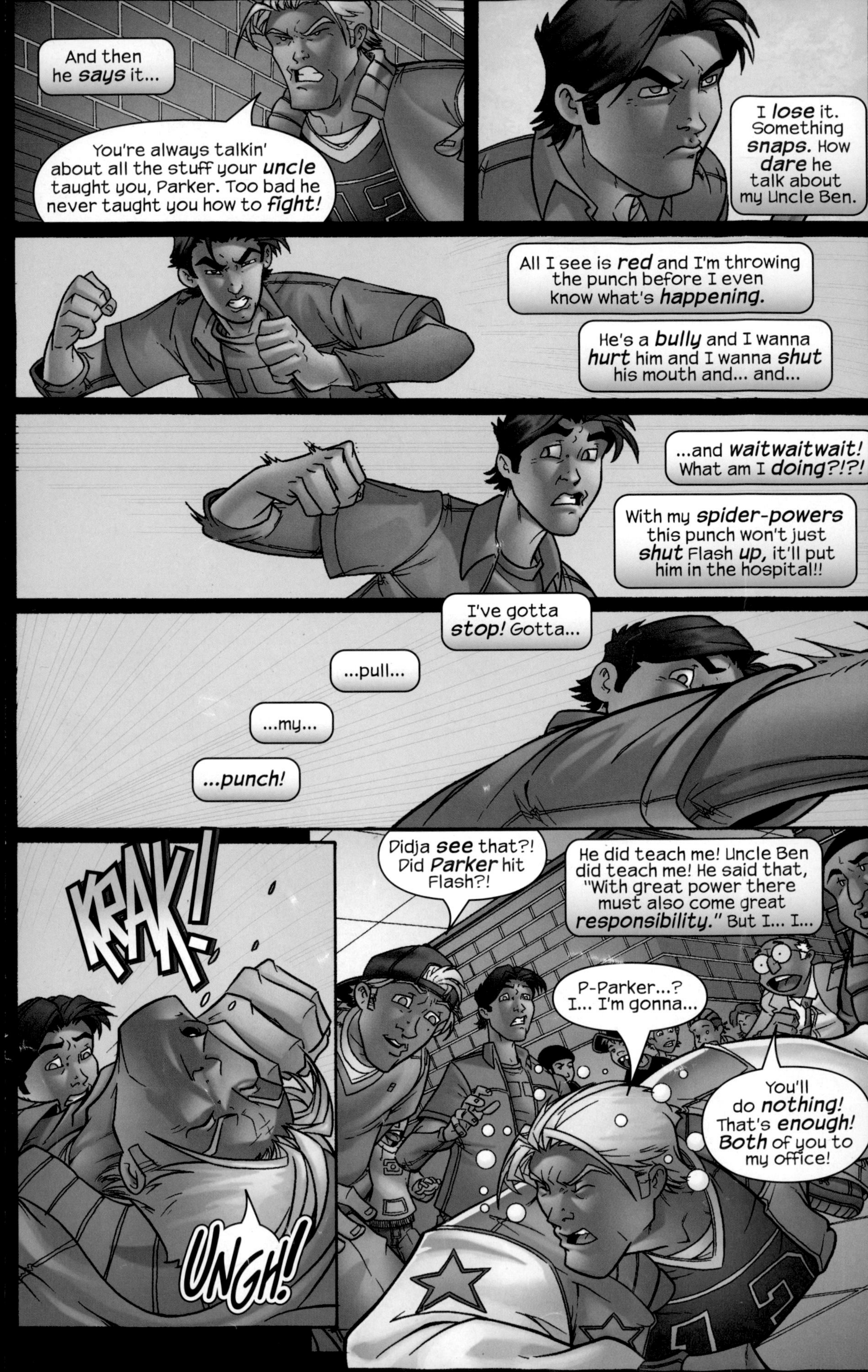
And then he *says* it...
You're always talkin' about all the stuff your *uncle* taught you, Parker. Too bad he never taught you how to *fight!*
I *lose* it. Something *snaps.* How *dare* he talk about my Uncle Ben.
All I see is *red* and I'm throwing the punch before I even know what's *happening.*
He's a *bully* and I wanna *hurt* him and I wanna *shut* his mouth and... and...
...and *waitwaitwait!* What am I *doing?!?!*
With my *spider-powers* this punch won't just *shut* Flash *up,* it'll put him in the hospital!!
I've gotta *stop!* Gotta...
...pull...
...my...
...punch!
KRAK!
UNGH!
Didja *see* that?! Did *Parker* hit Flash?!
He did teach me! Uncle Ben did teach me! He said that, "With great power there must also come great *responsibility.*" But I... I...
P-Parker...? I... I'm gonna...
You'll do *nothing!* That's *enough!* *Both* of you to my office!

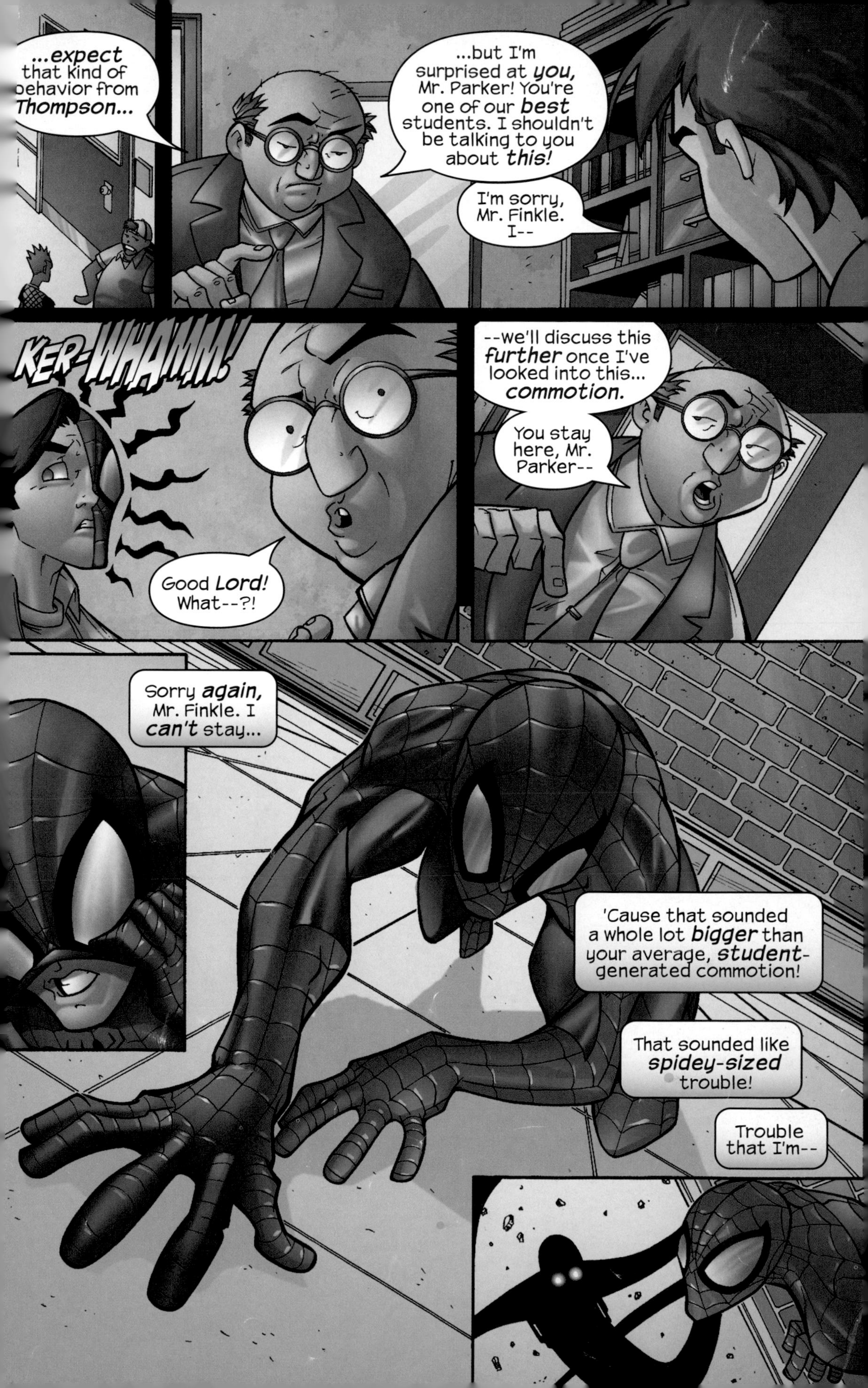
...expect that kind of behavior from Thompson...
...but I'm surprised at you, Mr. Parker! You're one of our best students. I shouldn't be talking to you about this!
I'm sorry, Mr. Finkle. I--
KER-WHAMM!
Good Lord! What--?!
--we'll discuss this further once I've looked into this... commotion.
You stay here, Mr. Parker--
Sorry again, Mr. Finkle. I can't stay...
'Cause that sounded a whole lot bigger than your average, student-generated commotion!
That sounded like spidey-sized trouble!
Trouble that I'm--

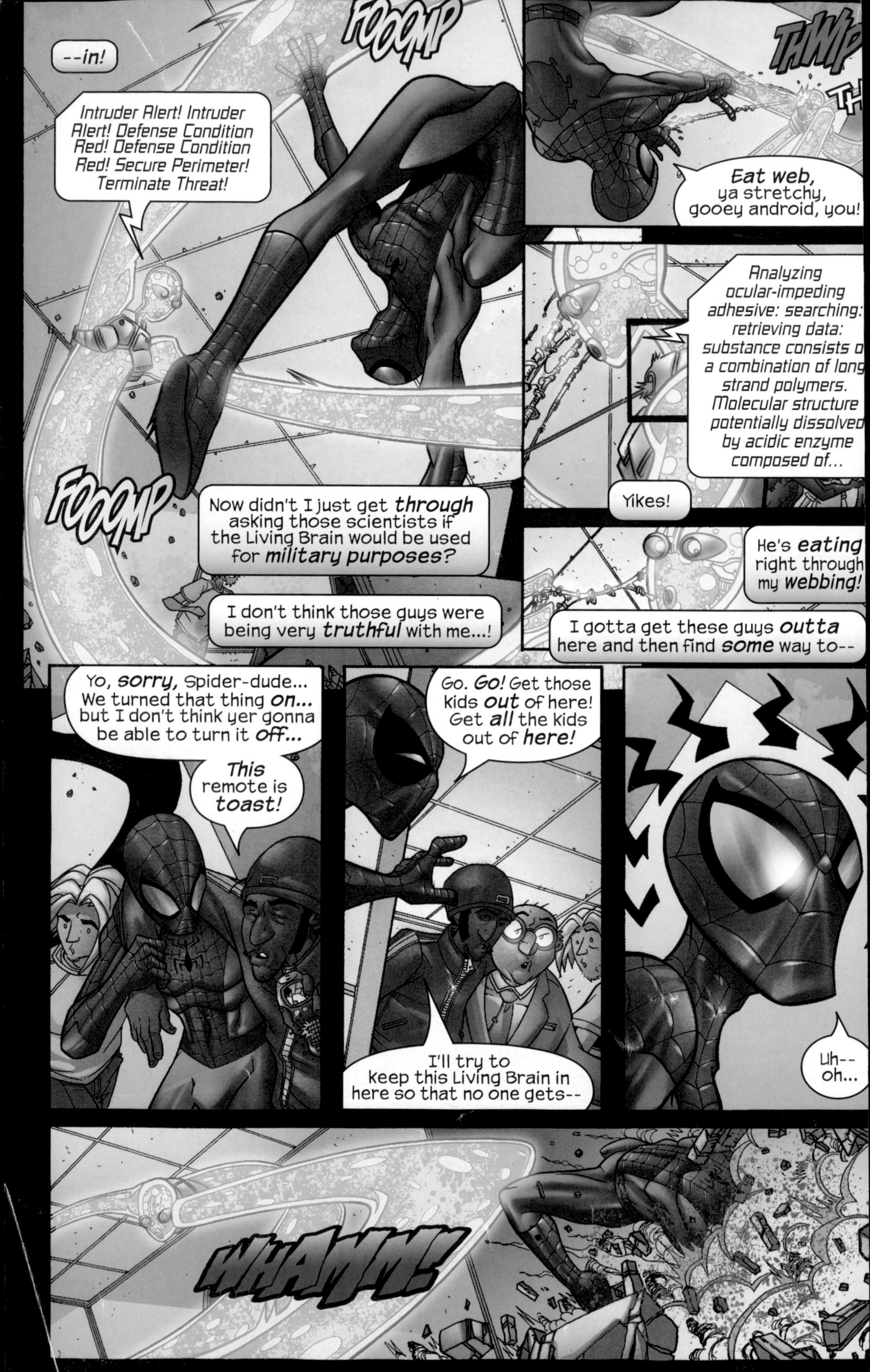
--in!
FOOOMP
Intruder Alert! Intruder Alert! Defense Condition Red! Defense Condition Red! Secure Perimeter! Terminate Threat!
FOOOMP
Now didn't I just get through asking those scientists if the Living Brain would be used for military purposes?
I don't think those guys were being very truthful with me...!
THWIP
Eat web, ya stretchy, gooey android, you!
Analyzing ocular-impeding adhesive: searching: retrieving data: substance consists o a combination of long strand polymers. Molecular structure potentially dissolved by acidic enzyme composed of...
Yikes!
He's eating right through my webbing!
I gotta get these guys outta here and then find some way to--
Yo, sorry, Spider-dude... We turned that thing on... but I don't think yer gonna be able to turn it off...
This remote is toast!
Go. Go! Get those kids out of here! Get all the kids out of here!
I'll try to keep this Living Brain in here so that no one gets--
Uh-- oh...
WHAMM!

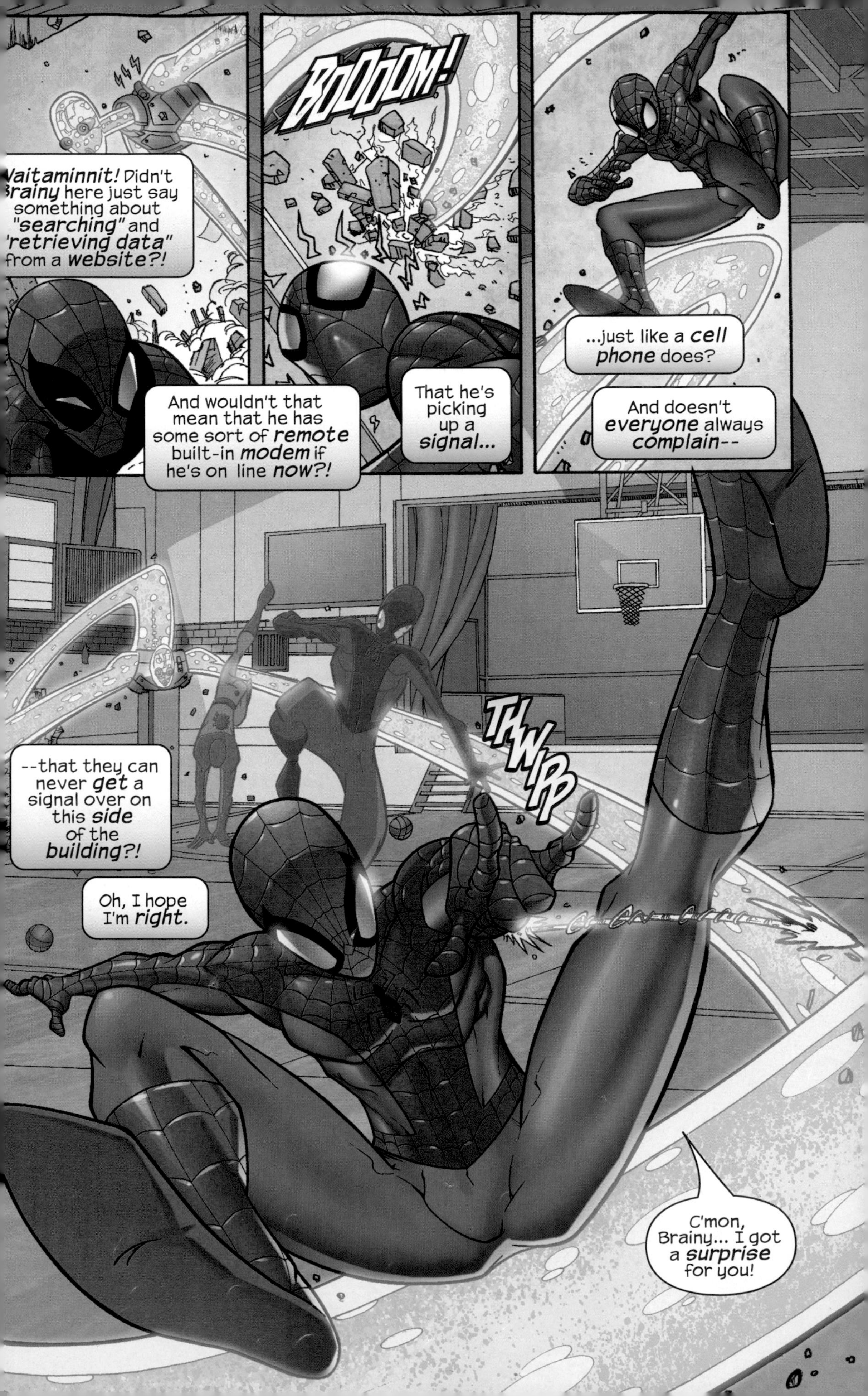

Waitaminnit! Didn't Brainy here just say something about "searching" and "retrieving data" from a website?!
And wouldn't that mean that he has some sort of remote built-in modem if he's on line now?!
BOOOOM!
That he's picking up a signal...
...just like a cell phone does?
And doesn't everyone always complain--
THWIPP
--that they can never get a signal over on this side of the building?!
Oh, I hope I'm right.
C'mon, Brainy... I got a surprise for you!

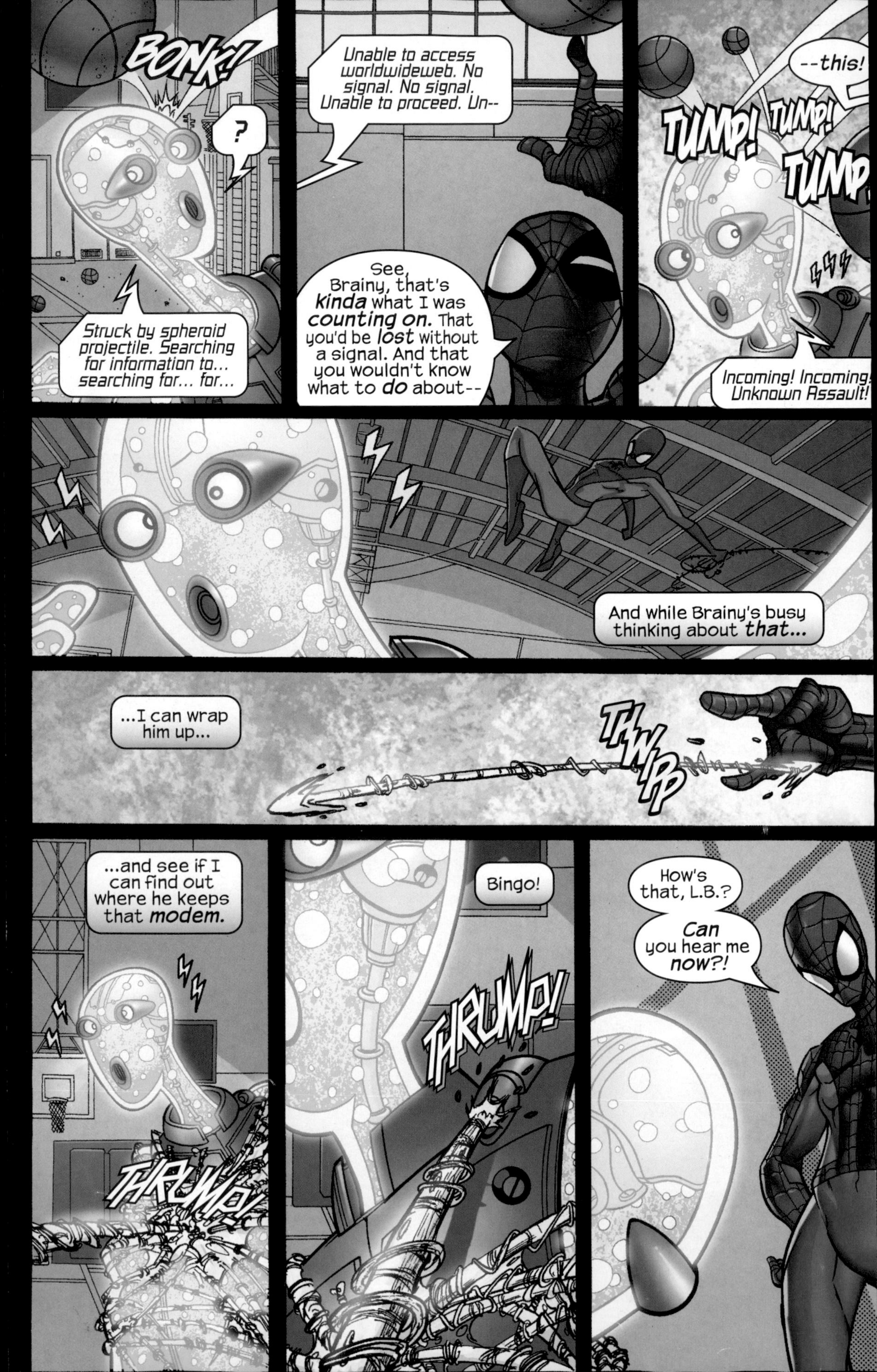
BONK!
?
Struck by spheroid projectile. Searching for information to... searching for... for...
Unable to access worldwideweb. No signal. No signal. Unable to proceed. Un--
See, Brainy, that's kinda what I was counting on. That you'd be lost without a signal. And that you wouldn't know what to do about--
--this!
TUMP! TUMP! TUMP!
Incoming! Incoming! Unknown Assault!
And while Brainy's busy thinking about that...
...I can wrap him up...
THWIPP
...and see if I can find out where he keeps that modem.
THRUMP!
Bingo!
THRUMP!
How's that, L.B.?
Can you hear me now?!

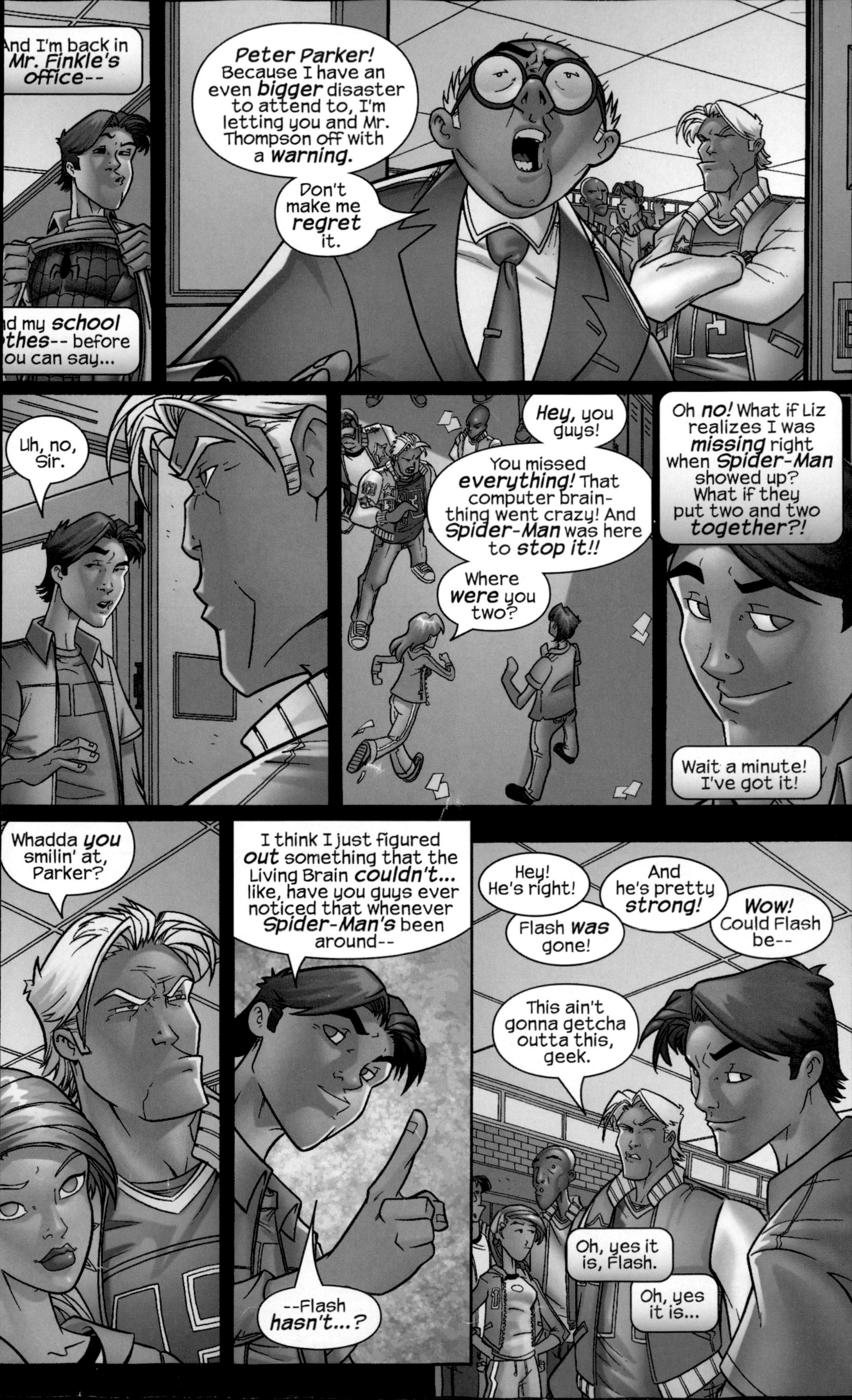
And I'm back in Mr. Finkle's office--
nd my school thes-- before ou can say...
Peter Parker! Because I have an even bigger disaster to attend to, I'm letting you and Mr. Thompson off with a warning.
Don't make me regret it.
Uh, no, Sir.
Hey, you guys!
You missed everything! That computer brain-thing went crazy! And Spider-Man was here to stop it!!
Where were you two?
Oh no! What if Liz realizes I was missing right when Spider-Man showed up? What if they put two and two together?!
Wait a minute! I've got it!
Whadda you smilin' at, Parker?
I think I just figured out something that the Living Brain couldn't... like, have you guys ever noticed that whenever Spider-Man's been around--
--Flash hasn't...?
Hey! He's right!
Flash was gone!
And he's pretty strong!
Wow! Could Flash be--
This ain't gonna getcha outta this, geek.
Oh, yes it is, Flash.
Oh, yes it is...

Well, I hate to *admit* it... but Flash is *right*...

I *am* a geek.

I love to *study*, I don't fit in... and every time I try to even say *hello* to Liz-- or any *other* girl-- I feel like I've got a mouth fulla *web-fluid!*

I wish I could be *cool*... like...

Hey, there's that new *Teen Center* the *Fantastic Four* put together!

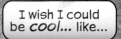

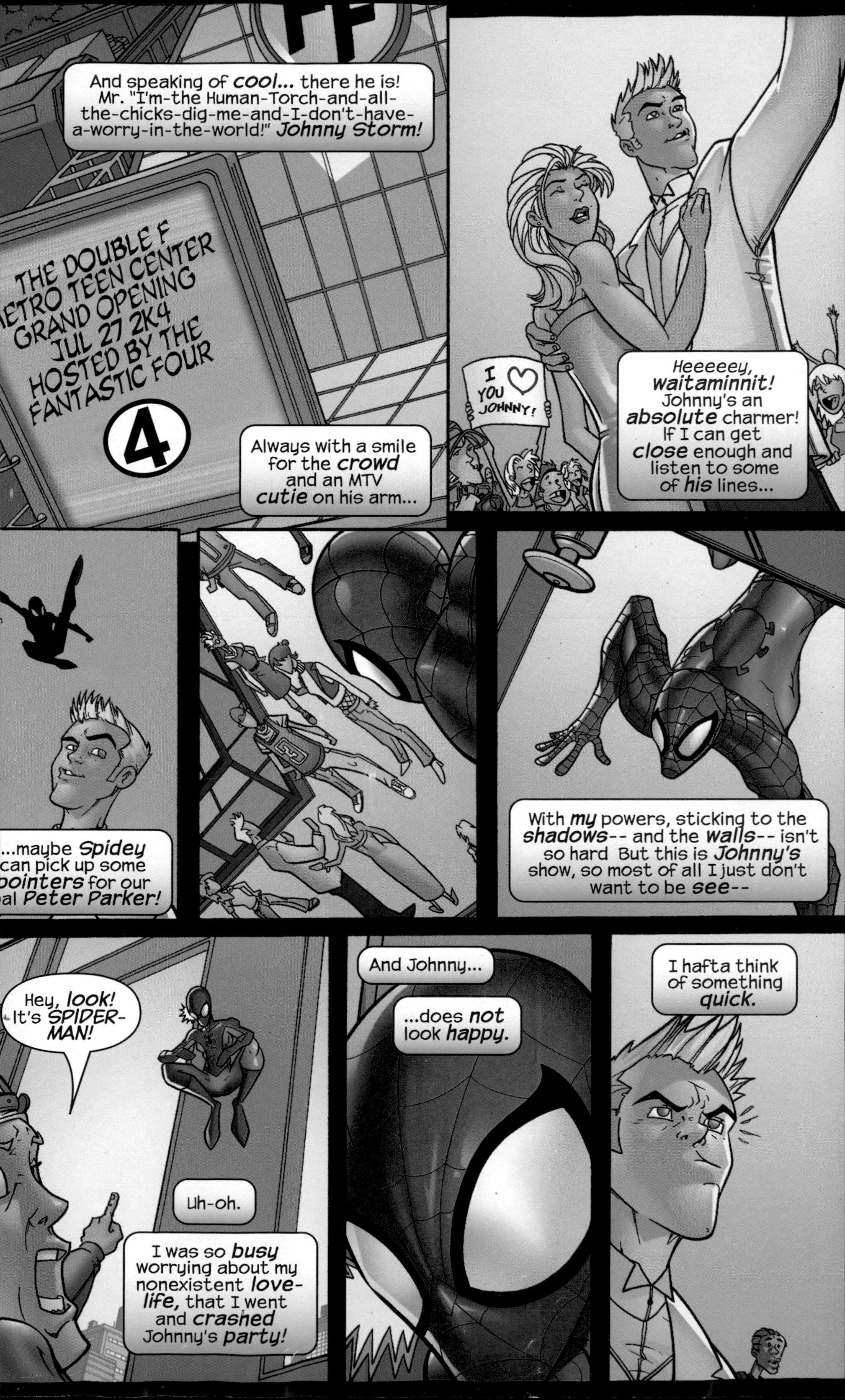

And speaking of cool... there he is! Mr. "I'm-the Human-Torch-and-all-the-chicks-dig-me-and-I-don't-have-a-worry-in-the-world!" Johnny Storm!
THE DOUBLE F
METRO TEEN CENTER
GRAND OPENING
JUL 27 2K4
HOSTED BY THE
FANTASTIC FOUR
4
Always with a smile for the crowd and an MTV cutie on his arm...
I ♡ YOU JOHNNY!
Heeeeey, waitaminnit! Johnny's an absolute charmer! If I can get close enough and listen to some of his lines...
...maybe Spidey can pick up some pointers for our pal Peter Parker!
With my powers, sticking to the shadows-- and the walls-- isn't so hard But this is Johnny's show, so most of all I just don't want to be see--
Hey, look! It's SPIDER-MAN!
Uh-oh.
I was so busy worrying about my nonexistent love-life, that I went and crashed Johnny's party!
And Johnny...
...does not look happy.
I hafta think of something quick.

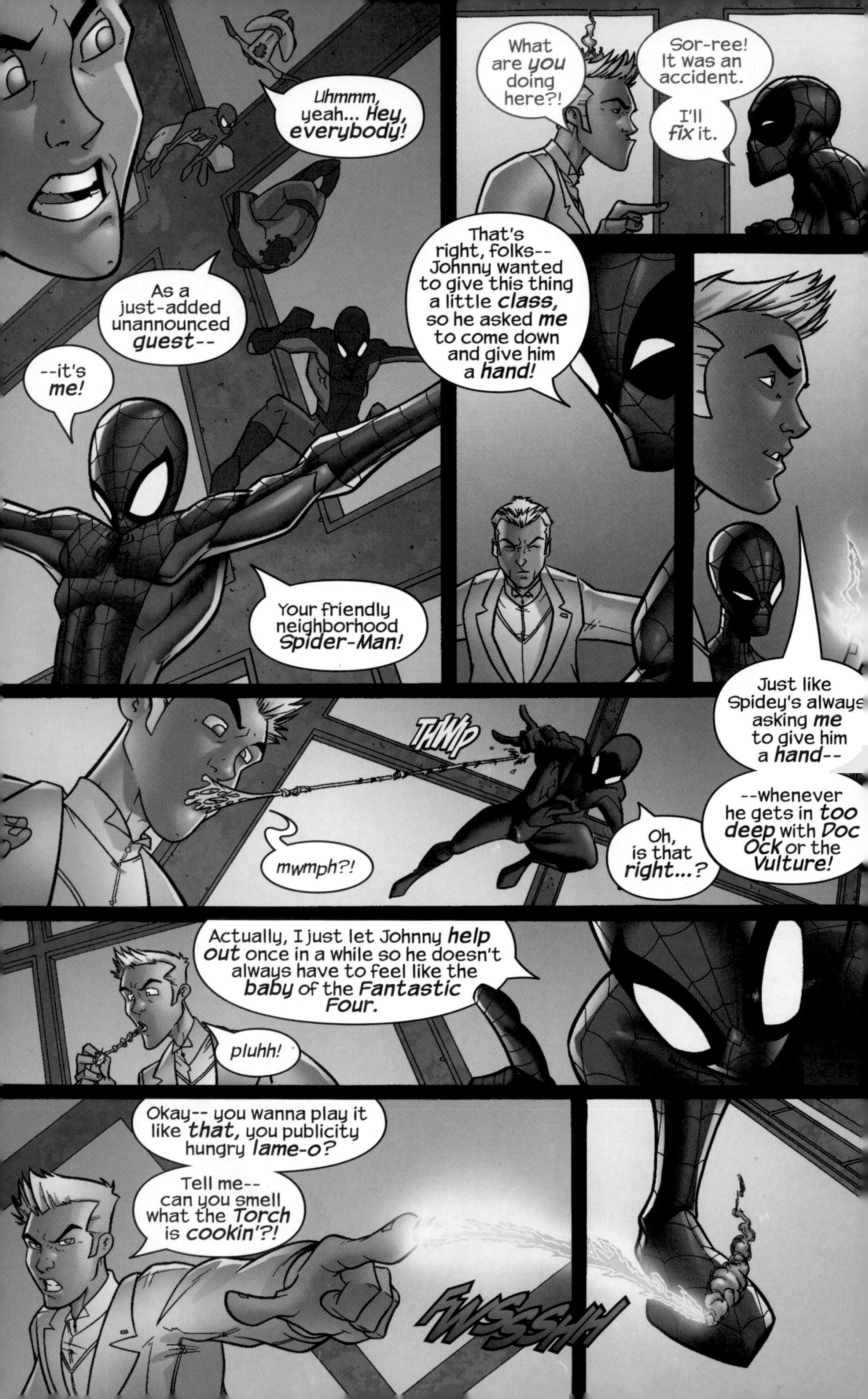
Uhmmm, yeah... Hey, everybody!
As a just-added unannounced guest--
--it's me!
Your friendly neighborhood Spider-Man!
What are you doing here?!
Sor-ree! It was an accident.
I'll fix it.
That's right, folks-- Johnny wanted to give this thing a little class, so he asked me to come down and give him a hand!
Just like Spidey's always asking me to give him a hand--
--whenever he gets in too deep with Doc Ock or the Vulture!
THWIP
mwmph?!
Oh, is that right...?
Actually, I just let Johnny help out once in a while so he doesn't always have to feel like the baby of the Fantastic Four.
pluhh!
Okay-- you wanna play it like that, you publicity hungry lame-o?
Tell me-- can you smell what the Torch is cookin'?!
FWSSSH

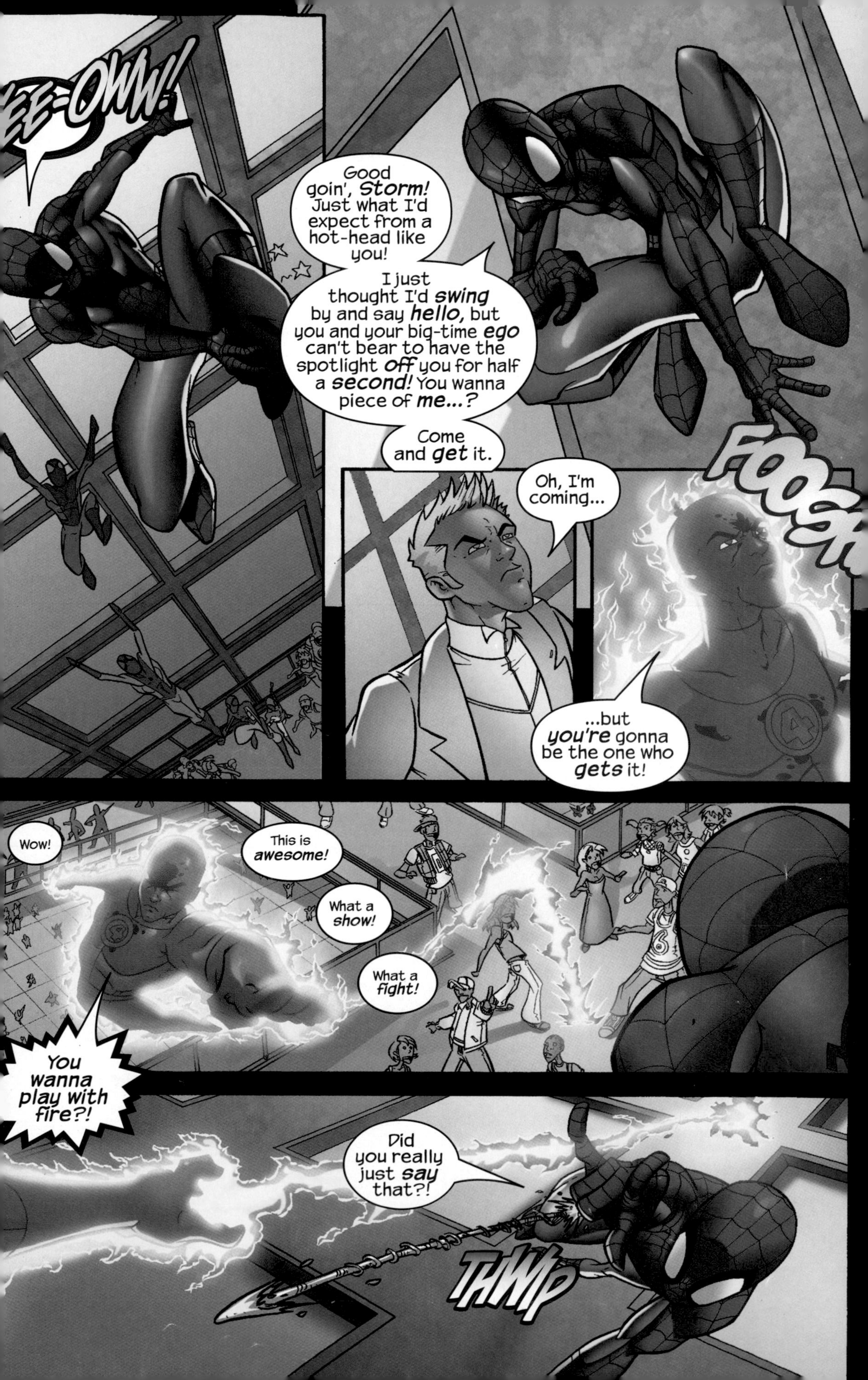

EE-OWW!
Good goin', Storm! Just what I'd expect from a hot-head like you!
I just thought I'd swing by and say hello, but you and your big-time ego can't bear to have the spotlight off you for half a second! You wanna piece of me...?
Come and get it.
Oh, I'm coming...
FOOSH
...but you're gonna be the one who gets it!
Wow!
This is awesome!
What a show!
What a fight!
You wanna play with fire?!
Did you really just say that?!
THWIP

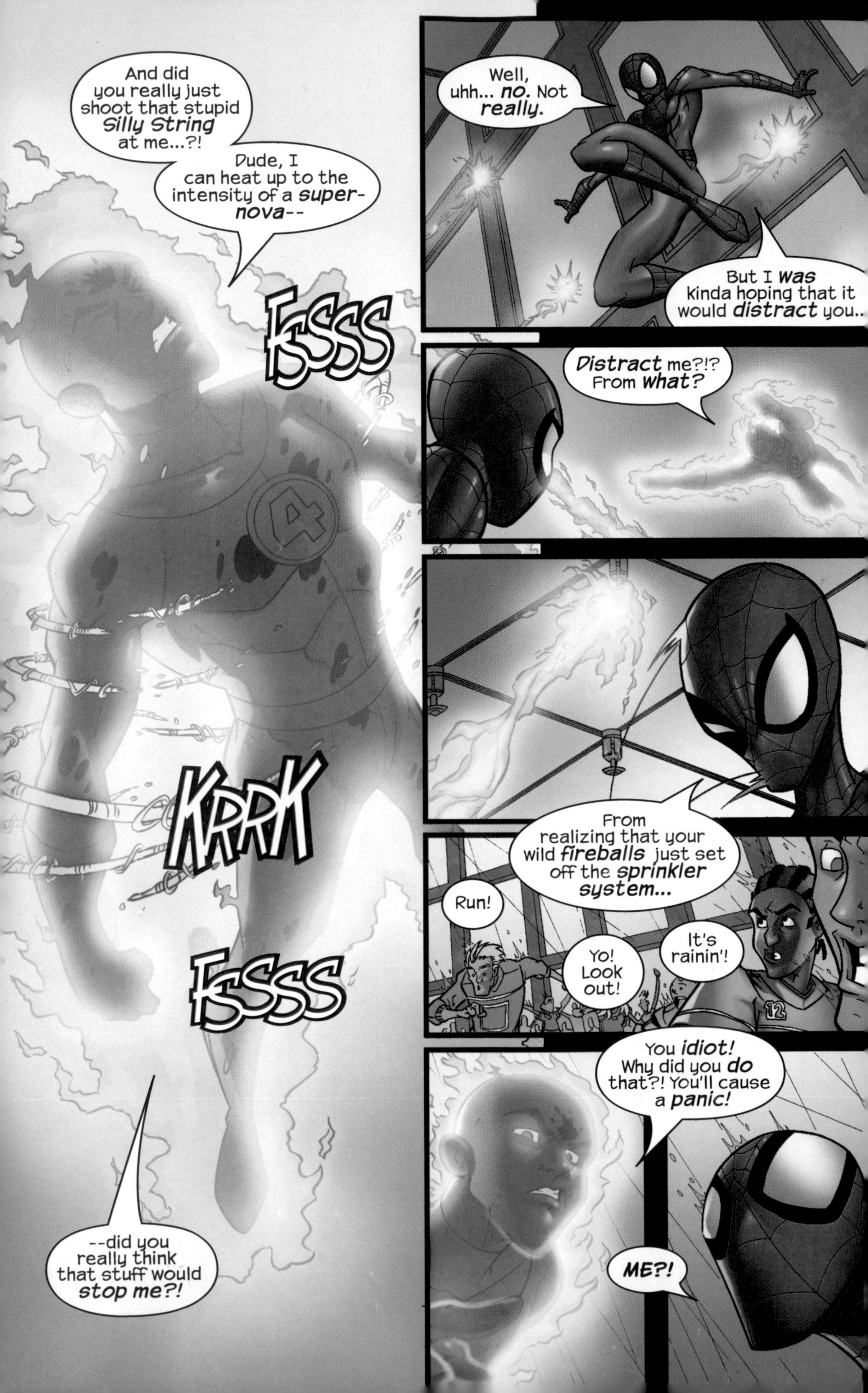
And did you really just shoot that stupid Silly String at me...?!
Dude, I can heat up to the intensity of a super-nova--
FSSSS
KRRK
FSSSS
--did you really think that stuff would stop me?!
Well, uhh... no. Not really.
But I was kinda hoping that it would distract you...
Distract me?!? From what?
From realizing that your wild fireballs just set off the sprinkler system...
Run!
Yo! Look out!
It's rainin'!
You idiot! Why did you do that?! You'll cause a panic!
ME?!

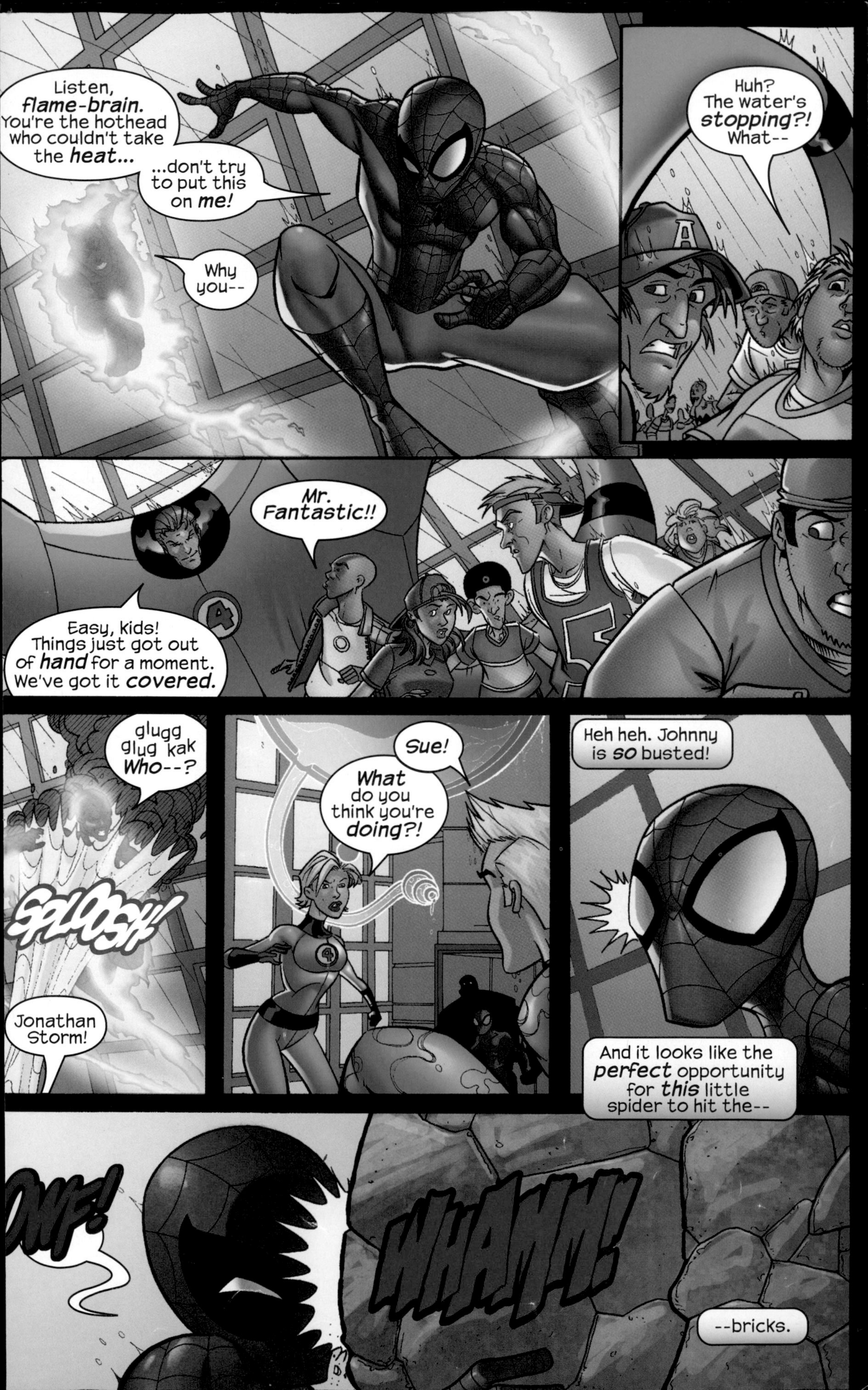
Listen, flame-brain. You're the hothead who couldn't take the heat...
...don't try to put this on me!
Why you--
Huh? The water's stopping?! What--
Mr. Fantastic!!
Easy, kids! Things just got out of hand for a moment. We've got it covered.
glugg glug kak Who--?
SPLOOSH!
Jonathan Storm!
Sue!
What do you think you're doing?!
Heh heh. Johnny is SO busted!
And it looks like the perfect opportunity for this little spider to hit the--
OWF!
WHAMM!
--bricks.

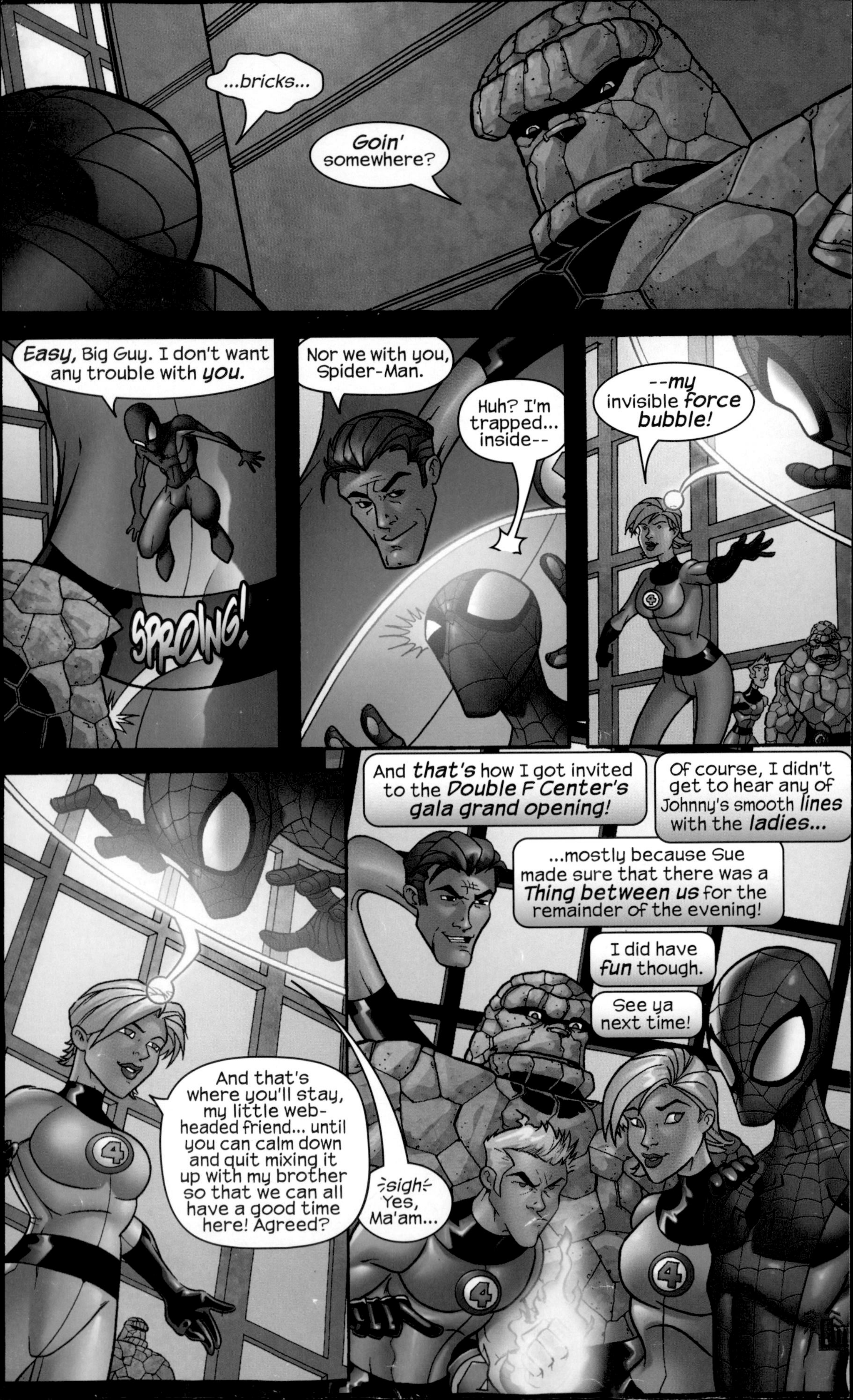
...bricks...
Goin' somewhere?
Easy, Big Guy. I don't want any trouble with you.
SPROING!
Nor we with you, Spider-Man.
Huh? I'm trapped... inside--
--my invisible force bubble!
And that's where you'll stay, my little web-headed friend... until you can calm down and quit mixing it up with my brother so that we can all have a good time here! Agreed?
sigh Yes, Ma'am...
And that's how I got invited to the Double F Center's gala grand opening!
Of course, I didn't get to hear any of Johnny's smooth lines with the ladies...
...mostly because Sue made sure that there was a Thing between us for the remainder of the evening!
I did have fun though.
See ya next time!